THE TRUE SPIRIT OF CHRISTMAS

AMISH CHRISTMAS ROMANCE

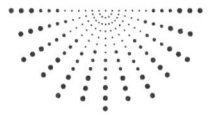

SARAH MILLER

SWEETBOOKHUB.COM

CHAPTER ONE

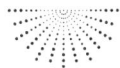

FAITH'S CREEK, PENNSYLVANIA.

"Can you believe how much she's grown?" Beth Phillips said, as her husband Isaac entered the house.

He smiled at her and their daughter, Louisa, who now looked up from the kitchen workbench where she had been *helping* Beth with the Christmas baking. They had been making bread, and Louisa – along with most of the kitchen and Beth – were covered in flour.

"*Daed...da*, helping," she said, and Isaac laughed.

"I can see that. What have you been making?" he asked, coming to put his arms around her and lifting her off the workbench.

"Bread and cakes," she said,

Beth, smiled at such a wonderful sight. "They should taste all right – even if there's a mess to clear up. Sit yourself down, I'll make you some coffee."

"*Denke*," he said sinking to a seat with Louisa still on his knee.

"Did you get all the wood chopped?" she asked, glancing out of the window toward the woodpile, which was already covered in snow.

It had been snowing in Faith's Creek for three days solid, it looked like the run-up to Christmas was bringing with it the wintry weather. Beth liked it like this – she liked stoking up the stove and making casseroles and baking bread. She had her Christmas crafts to make and sell, and there was always someone popping in to pass the time of day. Isaac divided his time between work on their smallholding and a job laboring on one of the local farms. Beth had her hands full looking after Louisa, who, at two years old, was growing ever more boisterous and interested in the world around her. But she would not have it any other way – she loved her life in Faith's Creek, and all the joys it brought.

"I got most of it done. And I covered up the potato sacks in the outhouse. The snow was blowing in through that break in the window. I wish I'd repaired it after that bird flew into it," Isaac replied, sitting down on a chair by the stove.

"You can't do everything. Here, try one of these – Louisa insisted on making it for you," Beth said, handing Isaac an oddly shaped bun studded with currants which she had liberally dusted with sugar to make it slightly more appealing.

"I made it, Daedda," Louisa said.

Isaac took it wide-eyed. "Then I'm sure it'll be delicious, sweetheart," he replied, taking a bite.

"Don't forget, we've got Kathryn coming for dinner tonight. I'm making buttered noodles and a shoofly pie. I'll put Louisa down for a nap shortly, then get her up to see her *grossmammi* before she goes to bed. You know how much Kathryn loves seeing her." Beth poured a cup of coffee for Isaac.

He put Louisa down.

Kathryn was Louisa's *grossmammi*, the *mamm* of Irene, who in turn was the *mamm* of Louisa. She was living out west and had no intention of ever returning to Faith's Creek, she had signed the adoption papers, and made Beth and Isaac the parents of her baby, born out of wedlock, and to a man who had simply disappeared in neglect of his responsibilities. Beth knew how much Kathryn missed her daughter, and she had tried to involve the older woman in every aspect of Louisa's upbringing. Kathryn doted on her granddaughter, and Louisa loved her *grossmammi* in return.

"Oh, sorry, yes, it slipped my mind," Isaac said.

Louisa came crawling across the floor and clambered up onto his knee.

"You don't need to worry – she's coming at seven o'clock, and I've got everything ready," Beth replied.

She had been busy that day – not only with her baking but with preparations for her craft stall at the Christmas market which was to take place on the weekend before the holidays. Christmas was Beth's favorite time of year – the excitement building, the school pageant, the happy and expectant faces, not to mention the snow, which carpeted the landscape around Faith's Creek and made everything appear fresh and new.

"I'm glad Kathryn can be involved with Louisa. It's so sad what happened – with Irene, I mean," Isaac said, bouncing Louisa on his knee.

"She called in this morning for coffee – just as I was getting Louisa dressed after you left for work. She had some interesting news," Beth replied.

"Oh, yes? What sort of news?" he asked.

"Well, it's sad, really, but she has a niece out in Pittsburgh – she lost her husband a few months back. She's spoken of her before. Her name's Trina. Well, she's coming to Faith's Creek for the holidays, so we'll be meeting her," Beth replied.

"Poor her, how old is she?" Isaac said, shaking his head.

"Only thirty-two. It was such a tragedy – he died in a car crash. I remember Kathryn mentioning it. She went out there for the funeral. There's a *boppli*, too, a toddler, I suppose, he's three years old, Andy's his name. Kathryn's going to have her hands full over the holidays, but we can all do our bit to make them welcome. If Faith's

Creek can do one thing well, it's hospitality," Beth replied.

She had been thinking a lot about Trina that day. She did not know her – only from what Kathryn had told her – but the thought of her at such a young age left a widow and with a *boppli*, too. It was so sad, and this being her first Christmas alone, Beth hoped she could do something to relieve the sorrow which Trina would certainly be feeling. She remembered how Christmas had once made her feel sad, too. Before Louisa, Beth had given up hope of ever being a *mamm*, and the thought of happy families at Christmas time had always made her weep. But all that was changed now, and Beth was certain she could do something to make this Christmas a happy one for them all.

"It certainly does – they'll fit right in, I'm sure. There's the pageant, the Christmas market, the service – they'll not have time to stop, and Trina won't be alone for a moment," Isaac replied.

"It'll do Kathryn good, too. She misses Irene so much. I know she's settled out west, but it's not the same. She's said goodbye to Faith's Creek, and that's that – she won't be coming back, but I don't think Kathryn can accept that," Beth said, shaking her head sadly.

"But don't forget, if it weren't for you, she'd not have Louisa, either. That's why it's so important to keep that link up. She dotes on her. That's her way of coping. When I saw her in the market the other day, she was buying wool – I think Louisa's going to have enough knitwear to last until she can knit it herself," he said, laughing, as Louisa looked up at the mention of her name.

"She couldn't ask for a better *grossmammi*. Well, I'd better finish dinner – would you set the table for us. I'll put Louisa down for a nap in a moment. She's getting groggy by the looks of it," Beth said.

The house was snug and cozy, a fire was burning in the stove, and the smell of cooking wafted through the parlor. Beth took Louisa in her arms and laid her in her day cot at the side of the room, smiling down at her, as her daughter gazed up in return and gave a gurgly smile.

"We're so lucky, aren't we?" Isaac said, coming to stand behind her and looking over her shoulder at Louisa, who gave an enormous yawn.

His beard brushed against her cheek – a reminder of his status as a married man, and she smiled as he put his arms around her waist and kissed her on the cheek

"The luckiest, and that's why I want to do all I can to make Trina welcome in Faith's Creek," Beth replied.

"Then let's invite her for dinner – we can tell Kathryn tonight. I've never known anyone to refuse a bowl of your buttered noodles," Isaac replied.

Beth thought that was a very good idea, indeed.

CHAPTER TWO

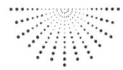

"Well, Andy, here we are," Trina Peachey said, gazing out over the snowy landscape around Faith's Creek from the window of the Greyhound bus.

It had been a long day, leaving Pittsburgh in the early hours when it was still dark and traveling across the state over endless miles of freeway. It was a long time since Trina had last visited her aunt *out in the sticks* as she referred to it, and the memories of happier days came flooding back.

In her childhood, Faith's Creek had meant holidays, ice creams, and endless days of sunshine, playing in the woods and by the creek. Trina had never visited in winter, and the snow and ice seemed a fitting accompaniment to the sadness she brought with her.

It had been three months since Melvin's accident, though it felt like only a moment ago that the terrible news had arrived. That moment would forever leave a dreadful wound, one which Trina was certain she could never recover from. It had been an accident, a car turning out of the road end at a faulty set of lights. Melvin had just been in the wrong place at the wrong time. The pain was unimaginable, and at one point Trina had wondered if she would ever stop crying. The tears came easily, and she was glad now of the distraction which a new place would bring, even as she dreaded the arrival of Christmas, a time when happiness was expected.

"Faith's Creek," the driver called out.

Trina struggled with her bags, holding Andy in her arms, as the doors of the bus slid open.

The bus stopped by a sign pointing down a lane between what, in the summer, were cornfields. Now they were harvested, bare, covered in snow, and looking a little desolate, just like her heart.

A buggy was pulled up across the way, the horse stomping its hooves in the cold, and Trina could see her aunt Kathryn waiting for her. She had aged somewhat since Trina had last seen her, her face worn, for they had both experienced trauma in the past year – the disappearance of Irene out west, Trina knew, caused her aunt much heartache. But now she smiled, holding out her arms to Trina and Andy and calling out a greeting.

"I timed it just right – I stopped at the bakery on the way and got here not five minutes ago. Well, it was Victor who drove me," she said, as a man Trina did not recognize appeared from behind the buggy.

He was about the same age as Trina's aunt, with fiery red hair, but clean-shaven, wearing a large overcoat against the cold.

"I'm pleased to meet you, Trina. I've heard a lot about you from your aunt. Welcome back to Faith's Creek," he said, stepping forward to take her bags.

Trina thanked him and embraced her aunt, who took Andy in her arms and kissed him.

"Haven't you grown, my little soldier? Oh, he looks just like Melvin," she said, and Trina nodded, smiling, even as the words brought tears to her eyes.

"A lot of people say that – he's got his eyes, big and blue. That's how I'll always remember Melvin," she replied.

"I know it won't be easy – Christmas, I mean – but you're here now, and we'll look after you. And there's Beth and Isaac, too, you remember them? They're Louisa's adopted parents, you'll meet them properly later on," Kathryn said.

Trina nodded, fighting off her fatigue as she climbed into the buggy and her aunt passed Andy up into her arms.

Trina knew all about what had happened with her cousin, Irene, of course. How she had gone off to Philadelphia and met a man who was far from what he had seemed – the man had taken advantage in the worst possible way and her pregnancy was a source of scandal in a place like Faith's Creek. It had been a terrible tragedy, but one which had produced something beautiful, a baby, innocent and pure. Trina had been greatly relieved to hear that Louisa was being well taken care of.

"I'm looking forward to meeting them. They must be really good people to make such a sacrifice," Trina replied, as Victor geed off the horses and the buggy pulled off down the snowy lane toward Faith's Creek.

"I'd be lost without them, and having Louisa here… it's such a blessing," Kathryn said.

"And what about you, Victor? What do you do to make ends meet?" Trina asked, curious to know more about her aunt's new friend.

Her aunt had mentioned Victor on several occasions in her letters, but Trina had not liked to pry as to who the man was. He seemed extremely nice, and Trina was glad that whatever the nature of their relationship, her aunt had someone to keep her company, particularly during the long, harsh Pennsylvanian winter.

"I'm about to open a café in the center of Faith's Creek. Just a small place, but it's always been my ambition. I've been a farm laborer all my life, but I love meeting new people, and I'm not so bad in the kitchen, either. My *daed* passed away last year and I've come into a little bit of money – enough to start up the café, at least. We'll see how it goes," Victor replied.

"Well, I wish you good luck. We'll have to come for a coffee and a piece of cake once you get started, won't we?" Trina said, glancing at her aunt, who nodded and smiled.

"I'm so glad you're here, Trina. You've been through so much and…" Kathryn began, a tear rolling down her cheek.

"And so have you. I'm glad we can be together, especially at Christmas," Trina replied.

"You remind me so much of Irene – I suppose we're all from the same stock," Kathryn said, putting her hand on Trina's and smiling at her.

Andy let out a cry and began to wriggle in Kathryn's arms. She stood him up on her knees and bounced him up and down. He was restless and started to cry.

"Let him face forward. He might like to see the horse," Kathryn said.

Trina leaned forward and held Andy up so that he could peer over Victor's shoulder.

Victor looked back and smiled as Andy smiled and reached out toward the horse.

"Do you want to hold the reins, young man?" he asked.

Andy nodded.

Victor made a show of holding up the reins for Andy, who reached out and clapped. But as he did so, the buggy lurched to one side, and Trina shot forward, just catching Andy before he hit his head on the sill. They had hit a patch of black ice on the lane, and the horse had lost its footing, sending the buggy sliding this way and that. Kathryn, too, had fallen from her seat. Victor was trying desperately to regain control, as a splintering sound came from the undercarriage.

"Oh, my," Kathryn cried out, as again the buggy swerved to one side, and Andy began to wail.

"It's all right," Victor cried out, but the horse was losing its footing again, and the buggy was sent careening across the lane, swerving this way and that.

For a moment, Trina thought all was lost, the sound of splintering came again from the undercarriage. She uttered a prayer out loud, begging *Gott* for their deliverance.

"Hold on to Andy," Kathryn cried, throwing herself forward to catch the reins from Victor, who had fallen backward.

Trina did as she was told, clutching at Andy, whose wails filled the buggy.

They lurched again to the side, throwing them to the floor where Tina struck her head against the door. Dazed and confused, it was as though darkness had come over her, her eyes barely open, the cries of Kathryn and Victor seeming distant, memories of Melvin – of the horrible crash that had killed him – now playing out in her mind.

"If this is to be the end, may it be swift," she prayed, clutching at Andy, as her world went dark.

CHAPTER THREE

*A*aron Lehman liked it when the snows covered Faith's Creek in the winter. There was a deathly silence across the landscape, one he could remember from childhood, a soundscape which he found comforting, given it was his own the entire year-round. Aaron was profoundly deaf. He had lost his hearing in a work accident some years ago, and the sounds he had once taken for granted – the rustle of leaves in the forest, or the sound of the plow in the field were gone. But so, too, were words – and that was what Aaron missed the most. He had always liked to talk, be it passing the time of day with a neighbor or debating with Bishop Beiler over last week's sermon. But all of that had come to a sudden and tragic end. Sound was gone, and without it, Aaron's world was far poorer.

But bitterness had never been on Aaron's heart – he had always tried to make the most of what fate had given him, believing always that *Gott* had a purpose. In losing his hearing, Aaron had found a renewed love of reading and often noticed things that others did not – his sight was as sharp as any could be. He would take long walks around Faith's Creek, often visiting the library to read, for the signs were always very clear *no talking* – which suited Aaron just fine. That afternoon, he had been reading his Bible, the pages open on the story of the healing of the blind man, but his eyes had been drawn to the snow, falling steadily outside.

From his vantage point at the window, Aaron could see across the garden of the small cabin which he shared with his brother, Jeremiah. Jeremiah worked at the mercantile store just outside of Faith's Creek, and he was just returning from work, trudging up the garden path and pulling off his boots on the front porch. Despite not hearing any of this, Aaron knew what it sounded like. He could remember sounds, just not hear new ones, and his brother's routine had been one which Aaron had long known. The two of them had lived together ever since the death of their parents. Once, they had been three, for Aaron had a sister, Mercy, but she, too, had died, leaving Aaron heartbroken. It was she who had done so much for him after the accident, learning sign language, and taking time out from her job as a florist on the market to take care of him.

The door opened, and Jeremiah entered the cabin. He was dressed in a thick overcoat and a hat with earmuffs pulled down and buttoned under his chin. He pulled it off to reveal his dusty blond hair, flecks of snow falling from the hat onto the rug, where they melted immediately. Aaron had stoked up the fire and the cabin was warm – just how he liked it. His brother gave him a withering look, for Jeremiah hated spending money on logs, and would rather the cabin be cold, even in the depths of winter. He signed to Aaron, though the swiftness of his movements was too much, and Aaron had to gesture for him to repeat.

Why are you just sitting here? No food? he signed.

Jeremiah had never really bothered to learn sign language in detail. He gestured, and Aaron normally understood the meaning. He could lip read, too, though sometimes he mistook words, leading to awkward situations. It was hard, but Jeremiah did not help the situation. He had no patience, not like Mercy, and he expected Aaron to take on the brunt of the daily chores about the cabin. The pittance of an allowance that Jeremiah gave Aaron from their inheritance was barely enough to make ends meet, and from it, his brother expected Aaron to provide everything they needed.

I haven't been out to the store, Aaron signed back, and his brother grimaced.

I work. I don't have time. Go get something, Aaron signed, gesturing the last words with a jerk of his thumb.

Aaron nodded. There was no point in arguing with Jeremiah – it would only make him angrier, and having watched the snow through the window, Aaron thought it would be nice to walk in it. To feel the lightness of the snow falling around him, and to be amidst the silence of that magical snowy landscape. He pulled on his boots and put on an overcoat, glancing at himself in the mirror which hung by the door. Mercy always used to check her appearance before going out, and he pictured her now, her long, blonde hair flowing down her shoulders, and the smile she always gave him. He sighed, just as Jeremiah tapped him on the shoulder.

I'm going, Aaron signed, but his brother shook his head.

Don't be long, he replied, emphasizing the words by tapping on his watch.

Aaron made no reply, opening the door out onto the porch and stepping out into the snow. The garden, where in the summer the two brothers grew vegetables, was blanketed in drifts of snow, the path through only visible thanks to Jeremiah's boot prints. Aaron was pleased to escape the confines of the cabin, even if a walk to the grocery store was fraught with its own challenges, too. It was hard for him to communicate, a series of gestures given in response to the words he spoke – words he could not hear.

The cabin lay on the slopes of a hill leading up to a ridge overlooking Faith's Creek. In the summer, the slopes were blessed by sunshine, but in the winter, it was here that the bite of the wind seemed to hit the hardest. Aaron shivered, pulling his overcoat tightly around himself, and being careful not to slip on the ice which had formed on the surface of the lane. Several times, he almost slipped, the treacherous conditions seeming to worsen as he approached the bottom of the lane which forked left and right, one way leading to Faith's Creek, the other across the cornfields to where the main road leading north and south made its intersection.

Aaron could not remember the last time he had left Faith's Creek, it was not for many years, and amidst the limited world of sound, he found, too, a limitation on his ambitions and hopes. There was little he could hope for, save to continue the gentle life he lead, punctuated by the bi-weekly service and visits from those friends who remained loyal, despite the difficulties they faced in communication. There were times when Aaron wondered what life outside the community might be like for someone like him – he knew of devices that helped the deaf to communicate, computers and mobile phones, the ability to text and email, and though hearing aids were of no use given his absolute loss of hearing, he knew there were more practical ways to communicate than just by pen and paper.

But Aaron had grown up in the Amish community – it was all he had ever known – and the thought of stepping out of that, of abandoning its traditions simply to make his own life easier, was not a thought he entertained. In his own way, Aaron was happy, though there were times when he longed for companionship – not that of his brother or friends, but of a woman, someone who, like Mercy, would understand and accept him for who he was – the person he had become. Aaron was not bitter. He did not blame *Gott* for his afflictions, but he prayed that one day, happiness might find him, even in the most unexpected of circumstances.

It was a prayer that he knew his brother would laugh at. To Jeremiah, Aaron was useless.

His parents had lived in a house across the hillside, a rambling old place with a big veranda running on two sides, and which Aaron could see from his vantage point. The family that had bought it still maintained the tradition of erecting a large Christmas tree in the garden, and this was hung with oil lamps at night, glittering in the darkness. The afternoon was drawing on, and Aaron could see the owner – Benuel Miller – balancing on a ladder to hang them. The sight brought back happy memories, for it could have been his own *daed* there, hanging out the lanterns, as Aaron, Jeremiah, and Mercy watched from below. Mercy had always loved Christmas – it was her favorite time of the year, or so she used to say. She would always make him smile, and the two of them used to play together, the best of friends, as well as siblings.

At the bottom of the hill, Aaron was about to turn right, the grocery store being half a mile or so further down into the center of the community. Jeremiah liked pork chops on a Monday – it was his treat for finishing the first day back at work after the weekend. Aaron would cook them with mashed potatoes and root vegetables, just as his brother liked them. He felt guilty for not going shopping earlier, after all, Jeremiah did a lot for him – even if grudgingly. His brother was a good man at heart, but Aaron knew that he, too, was struggling, and making ends meet was becoming increasingly difficult. Aaron had just turned along the lane when a sight up ahead caused him to stop and look in horror.

There was buggy coming toward him, veering from side to side. The horse was panicking, losing its footing, and trying desperately to regain its balance as the buggy rocked from side to side. One of the wheels was splintered, and Aaron could see the desperate face of a man struggling with the reins. Aaron had heard of buggy accidents before – particularly in the snow and ice. It only took one foot wrong for a horse to get into difficulty in conditions like this. He ran forward in a desperate attempt to help the stricken buggy, which seemed almost certainly doomed to disaster...

CHAPTER FOUR

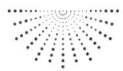

The buggy lurched again, and another splintering crack came from the undercarriage. Trina was dazed, her body wracked with pain from the fall to the floor, as she desperately tried to hold Andy out of harm's way.

Kathryn was shouting something to Victor, and the horse neighed as Trina tried to right herself, the buggy lurching sideways and coming to a sudden halt. For a moment, Trina closed her eyes, imagining something more disastrous to come, but there was only silence before Kathryn let out a sigh of relief.

"Oh, thank goodness, are you all right, Trina? Here, let me take Andy," Kathryn said.

Trina opened her eyes and struggled to sit up. Her head was aching, as was her body, but there was no permanent damage – as far as she could feel – and without Andy in her arms, she was able to pull herself up and sit back on the buggy seat with a sigh.

"I thought for a moment..." she began, glancing at her aunt, who shook her head.

"Don't think about what might have been. What matters is we're all right," Kathryn said, cradling Andy in her arms.

He was whimpering, the shock of what had happened evident on his face. Trina leaned forward and kissed him, whispering reassuringly in his ear.

"It's all right, you're safe, your *mamm* and great aunt are here," she said, putting her hand gently on the top of his head.

"We must have caught a patch of ice – Victor's seeing to the horse," Trina said.

Trina had completely forgotten about Victor in her haste to safeguard Andy, and now she glanced through the front of the buggy to see him standing with the horse, gesturing to a man dressed in a large overcoat and earmuffed hat.

"Who's the man he's with?" she asked, turning to her aunt.

Kathryn peered curiously over her shoulder. "Oh, it's Aaron Lehman – I wonder if…" she said, her words trailing off.

Victor was making strange gestures with his hands, and Trina wondered why the man was not answering, instead, he was shaking his head and staring blankly.

"He must have stopped the horse, somehow – I'm going to thank him," Trina said, and she opened the buggy door and clambered out.

Several of the wheel spokes had broken, but the buggy itself seemed undamaged. The horse was calm now, and Victor was stroking its neck, still gesturing to the man as Trina hurried over.

"We can't thank you enough – I've got my son in there, and if you hadn't come along and caught the horse – I presume you did – and, well, we can't thank you enough," she blurted out, the shock of what had happened only just taking hold.

They had come so near to disaster, and whatever her aunt might say about not thinking of what might have been, the thought of it brought tears to her eyes. She thought, too, of Melvin, and the terrible way in which he had died – cars scared her, and now she looked warily at the buggy, too, wondering if she would ever feel safe on the road again.

"Trina, this is Aaron Lehman. He lives not far from here. He did catch the horse's reins – we owe him our lives, or certainly our good health. I was nearly thrown out with that last lurch," Victor said.

Trina reached out and took the man by the hand and squeezed it gently.

"*Denke*, oh, *denke*," she said, but to her surprise, the man only looked at her blankly.

He nodded and gave a weak smile. He was handsome, perhaps thirty years old, with gray eyes and wisps of blond hair protruding from beneath the peak of his hat. He said something, but Trina could not understand it, and she glanced at Victor in confusion.

"Aaron is deaf, Trina. He had an accident some years ago. He can't hear what you're saying, but I'm sure he understands you mean to thank him for what he's done. We all owe him our thanks," Victor replied.

Trina felt suddenly embarrassed, and she looked Aaron straight in the face, trying to communicate by sight what she felt in her heart – the overwhelming gratitude of one who has come close to disaster and found themselves saved by another.

"I am... so grateful... to you," she said, mouthing the words in an exaggerated way.

"He understands," Victor said, patting Aaron on the arm.

Trina wished there was some way of thanking Aaron further, and she squeezed his hand once more, smiling at him, as he gazed at her, a smile coming over his face.

"You're welcome," he said, his voice sounding slightly out of sync, but clear, nonetheless.

Kathryn had climbed down from the carriage, holding Andy in her arms, and Trina pointed to him, glancing at Aaron, who smiled.

"This is my son, Andy," she said, gesturing to Aaron, and sounding out the name for him to understand, "A...n...d...y."

"Andy?" Aaron replied, and Trina nodded.

"That's right – you saved us all," she said, as her aunt came and took Aaron by the hand.

It was clear she knew better how to communicate with the man, and she handed Andy over to Trina before gesturing her thanks, always keeping her eyes fixed on Aaron so that he could read her lips clearly.

"Let us take you with us... we're having dinner soon," she said, and Aaron nodded.

"Invitation?" he asked, and Kathryn nodded.

"That's right – to thank you," she said, turning to Victor, who nodded.

"I'll lead the buggy. I won't risk driving it again – Conrad can take a look at it tomorrow and repair the spokes. It won't take much, but I'm wary of the ice, today," he said, and Kathryn nodded.

"I think we all are. But come on, we'll catch our death of cold if we stand out here any longer," she said, beckoning Trina and Aaron to follow her.

Trina glanced at Aaron, who seemed to understand he was being invited to share in a meal with them. It was the least they could do to thank him for what he had done that day. Trina smiled, nodding to Aaron, who smiled back.

"We'd like you to come," she said, gesturing at him, and he nodded.

"I will," he replied, and they climbed into the buggy after Kathryn, and Andy was placed in between them.

Andy had calmed down, his tears quietened, and Trina noticed he kept staring at Aaron curiously as Victor led the horse along the lane and the buggy moved slowly forward.

"It's all right, Andy. You can say "hello" to Aaron," she said.

Aaron looked up at her with wide, questioning eyes.

"He doesn't speak?" Andy asked.

Trina smiled. "He does speak – don't be rude, now. Some people have difficulty hearing but it's nothing to be afraid of. Aaron's ears are just a little broken, but he can understand – we can use gestures to talk to him. It's called sign language," Trina replied.

Andy looked up at Aaron, still with a puzzled expression.

Trina had known other deaf people in Pittsburgh. Before Melvin's death, she had volunteered at a home for the elderly, and there she had encountered those whose hearing had gone. She knew how important it was to make eye contact, to speak slowly and clearly, emphasizing the words so that the other could attempt to lipread, and though she had never learned formal sign language, she knew certain gestures to communicate at a basic level.

"Hello," Andy said, staring at Aaron, who smiled.

"Hello," he replied, and Andy turned to Trina in surprise, as though he had not been expecting such a response.

"You see, it's not hard to speak to someone, is it?" Trina said.

Andy shook his head.

Aaron was rummaging in his pocket, and he brought out a handful of sweets, wrapped in gold paper. They were toffees, and he offered one to Andy, who gazed at it in amazement. Trina did not, as a rule, allow Andy to have sweets, but the shock of what had happened, and the kindness of Aaron softened her heart and she nodded to Andy, who reached out his hand and took the sweet, unwrapping it as though it were a precious jewel, rather than a sticky toffee.

"*Denke*," Andy said, and Aaron smiled.

"You're welcome," he replied.

The buggy was turning into the gate of Kathryn's house, and Trina's aunt gestured to Aaron, telling him he must stay for dinner.

"I won't hear of a refusal. You've done a good deed today, Aaron, and I want to thank you. I'm going to tell Bishop Beiler what you did, and he'll be ever so proud," she said, through a mixture of signs and gestures, opening her mouth wide as she spoke.

They had pulled up outside the house, and Trina remembered it well from happy days in her childhood. The house was of wooden slats, set back from the road, and approached by a path through an orchard. The trees now bare and covered with snow looked magical and surreal. A path had been cleared up to the porch, and the windows were all lit with oil lamps, a welcoming sight in the gathering gloom of that wintery afternoon.

Trina was mightily relieved to have arrived, and all she wanted now was a hot meal and her bed – it had been a long day, one which could so easily have ended in disaster.

"That's it, safely home," Victor said, opening the door of the buggy and helping Kathryn out.

Trina was about to pass Andy to her aunt, but to her surprise, he wriggled free from her arms and launched himself onto Aaron, clinging to him in a tight embrace. She had never known him to behave like that. Aaron, too, looked down in surprise at the sight of Andy who now looked up and smiled.

"Thank you," he said, and Trina smiled.

"I think he likes you," she said, reaching out to pull Andy away, for he was clinging like a limpet to their new friend, who blushed and shook his head.

"I should go," he said, but Trina's aunt was hearing none of it.

"You'll stay – that brother of yours can fix his own dinner for once – you were on your way to the store, I'm sure. But tonight, we're looking after you," Kathryn said, beckoning Aaron to follow her.

He did not seem to entirely understand what Kathryn was saying, but he followed her out of the buggy and along the path up the steps to the porch. Trina followed with Andy, curious to know more about Aaron, and wondering what her aunt had meant by her words about his brother. Victor brought the bags, and at long last, Trina stepped into the warmth of the house, relieved to at last have completed her journey.

The house was just as Trina remembered it, warm and welcoming, filled with knickknacks and soft furnishings. There were cross-stitched pictures on the walls – scenes of Faith's Creek, and Pennsylvanian landscapes. Next to the door, a doll sat against the wall. It was a sad symbol, not for the subject, but for the memory. It had belonged to Irene, Trina's cousin, gone, but not forgotten. Trina looked up at it and sighed, remembering how they had played together as children. The last time she was here it was put away and she understood that Kathryn had got it out as a reminder of her daughter. A greeting came from behind.

"You must be Trina. We've heard so much about you."

Trina turned to find a woman cradling an infant in her arms, smiling at her from the entrance to the kitchen.

"Oh, you must be Beth," Trina said, having quite forgotten what her aunt had said about a welcoming committee.

"That's right, and this is my husband, Isaac," Beth replied, as a man emerged from the kitchen behind her with a smile on her face.

Just then, Kathryn and Aaron entered the parlor from the hallway where they had been hanging up coats and hats, and Beth looked surprised to see Aaron, who seemed somewhat embarrassed.

"What a terrible thing happened on the way back," Kathryn exclaimed, and with Victor's help, she told Beth and Isaac the story of the buggy and how they had come close to disaster.

Beth and Isaac listened in astonishment, and though Aaron could not hear, he knew when his part in the tale was recounted, for Kathryn turned to him and clutched her hands together, smiling at him with gratitude.

Victor came in at that moment, having taken care of the horse. "If it wasn't for Aaron here, we'd have had a nasty accident. The buggy would have overturned and… well," Victor said, shaking his head.

"You did well, Aaron," Isaac said, gesturing to him.

It was clear to Trina that Aaron was well known in Faith's Creek, and she glanced at him with a smile, noticing the blush coming over his face.

"He was a real hero – he ran straight over and grabbed the horse's reins. It settled him right down and meant I could regain control. There's not many in Faith's Creek who have that skill with a horse – not these days," Victor said, and he patted Aaron on the back.

"I've invited Aaron to stay for dinner – will you take him home later, Isaac?" Trina's aunt asked, and Isaac nodded.

"Certainly," he replied, and Aaron was ushered toward the kitchen where dinner was laid out on the table.

"I've made spice and applesauce cakes for dessert, and there's buttered noodles, baked potatoes, sliced ham, and pickles – just come and help yourselves," Beth said, and the others crowded round.

Aaron seemed hesitant, a nervous look coming over his face, and Trina turned to him and held out her hand.

"It's all right. Come and eat," she gestured, but Aaron shook his head, holding back, reluctance etched on his face.

CHAPTER FIVE

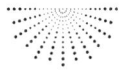

The sounds of crockery and cutlery clinking came from the kitchen, and there was much exclamation of delight at the food that Beth had prepared, but still, Aaron held back. Trina had Andy in her arms, and he was looking at Aaron, his head on one side, a curious expression on his face.

"Does he not eat?" Andy asked.

Trina smiled. "No, it's not that – he's just a little shy," she whispered, taking a step forward and offering her hand to Aaron once again.

"I'm hungry," Andy said, and as if on cue, his stomach rumbled.

"Come on now, let's not let it get cold," Kathryn called out, appearing from the kitchen to see where Trina and Aaron had got to.

"We'll be there in a moment," Trina said, turning to her aunt, who pointed back at the table.

"There's a place set for Aaron. He's the guest of honor," she replied, before disappearing back into the kitchen.

To Trina's surprise, it was Andy who broke the tension, holding out his arms to Aaron, who smiled.

"Come on," he said, and Trina held him out to Aaron, who took him in his arms and smiled.

"He's never normally like this – he likes you," Trina said, forgetting for a moment the difficulty Aaron would have in understanding her.

But the actions of Andy did not seem to need words, and the kindness of his gesture had wiped the nervous look from Aaron's face. Holding Andy in his arms, he followed Trina into the kitchen, where the others were tucking in. Beth had prepared a feast, and there were still yet more dishes to come – bread was proving on the side, and chicken waiting to be cooked on the stove.

"Oh, there you are – you've made a friend, Andy," Kathryn said, as they all took their seats at the table.

Andy seemed happy to sit on Aaron's lap, and Trina offered them both the platter of ham and beef. Louisa looked curiously up from her seat, fixing Andy and Aaron with a smile.

"You've got quite an audience there, Aaron," Isaac said, gesturing to the *kinner* and pointing at Aaron, who smiled.

"*Kinner* don't have the same kind of awkwardness we do – they ask questions, they're curious, and they accept people for the way they are. They can deal with differences – so long as they're explained. Grown-ups can learn a lot from watching them," Kathryn said, passing around the dish of baked potatoes.

Trina found it fascinating to watch how Andy responded to Aaron. Her aunt was right. He showed absolutely no fear, now that things had been explained to him. He was content to accept Aaron, and in turn, Aaron seemed totally at ease with him – more so than with the rest of them. Louisa, too, was watching in fascination and when Aaron pulled a silly face at her, she began to giggle, causing Andy to do so, too.

"Oh, look at them both, aren't they adorable?" Beth said, smiling as the two *kinner* continued to giggle.

"We're blessed to have Aaron here tonight – he's done something truly remarkable. I'm going to tell the whole of Faith's Creek about it," Kathryn said.

Victor shook his head. "I don't know if Aaron would want that, Kathryn. He's a private man, you know that."

Kathryn was adamant. "I'm going to tell Bishop Beiler – at the very least. He needs to know there's a hero amongst us," she said.

Trina smiled. Returning to Faith's Creek had certainly been dramatic if nothing else, and she would not forget it in a hurry. Pittsburgh seemed a long way away, the hustle and bustle of the city replaced by the quiet solitude of Faith's Creek, with its scattered dwellings and rolling, snow-covered landscape. It was good to be here, surrounded by the familiar and with her aunt, and the new friends she had made in Aaron, Beth, Isaac, and Victor. Trina had felt very alone in the city after Melvin's death, it was a loneliness that felt strange, given she was so surrounded by noise, but loneliness it was. Now she realized what she had been craving these long months past, the company of others, and the reassurance of something more.

"He's certainly that," she said, turning to her aunt, who nodded.

"I'd better shape those rolls – does everyone want bread?" Beth asked, pointing at the proving basket, where the dough had risen so far up it was almost spilling out.

Everyone nodded, but as Beth rose to her feet, Aaron did the same, still holding Andy in his arms he came to help her.

"He was always a good cook," Kathryn said, and Aaron gestured at Beth to let him do the work.

"Oh, you can't do it – you're our guest," she said, gesturing back at him, but he shook his head and smiled.

He sat Andy down on the worktop and rolled up his sleeves, flouring the work surface from an open bag on the side and taking a piece of dough, which he shaped into a round, followed by another and another. Beth smiled, glancing at Trina, who watched in fascination. Andy, too, was mesmerized, and Louisa was straining her neck to see, so much so that Isaac lifted her up and held her out to watch.

"A man of many talents," Kathryn remarked, and Trina smiled.

"He certainly is," she whispered, even though, with his back turned, Aaron would never have known what she was saying.

In no matter of time, a baking tray was covered in perfectly equal balls of dough. Aaron took a knife and cut a criss-cross into the top of each one before flouring it again. It did not take long for them to prove, and soon the kitchen was filled with the smell of freshly baking bread – surely one of the most delightful smells imaginable. Aaron was sitting back down at the table, and Andy had climbed onto his lap again as Beth prepared the chicken for cooking.

"I've never known a guest step in to cook, too. We owe you doubly, Aaron," Kathryn said.

Aaron smiled, though Trina could tell he did not quite understand what was being said to him.

He was certainly a remarkable man, and Trina was eager to learn more about him. She was so grateful to him for saving them, and though communication was difficult, she intended to try and understand him, for she had hoped to make friends in Faith's Creek, and already it seemed she had.

"That's the chicken ready, and I think the bread rolls, too," Beth said, opening the oven from which a plume of steam emerged.

She brought out the tray of rolls, all of them perfectly formed, risen uniformly, and with a rich, golden crust on top. They were a far cry from the cheap, nasty bread which Trina would buy in the grocery stores in Pittsburgh. Beth offered them around, and everyone complimented her on her baking.

"These are delicious, Beth," Victor said, taking a bite liberally spread with butter.

"But I'd never have been able to shape them as Aaron did," she admitted, glancing at Aaron, who nodded, pointing at the bread and smiling.

"Nice dough, soft and sweet," he replied.

"What a feast this is to welcome us here," Trina said, glancing around at the others.

Beth smiled. "Well, we want to make your stay here with us special. We know the awful time you've had and whilst a few bread rolls and a bit of chicken can't take that away, they can at least show you you're welcome here. We've got lots planned – there's the *kinner* pageant at the school, the church services, and Christmas day – we had a wonderful celebration last year, but it's so nice to think Louisa has someone to play with. I'm sure she and Andy will get on well."

Trina glanced at Andy, who clinging to Aaron had fallen fast asleep with his thumb in his mouth. It was quite remarkable, for Andy had become quite withdrawn since the death of his *daed*, and was often reluctant to leave Trina's side. It was natural, she had supposed, but to see him content brought joy to her heart, and she wondered if she, too, might find a similar peace here in Faith's Creek.

"Has everyone had enough?" Kathryn asked when the spice and applesauce cakes had been finished.

There was a murmur around the table, and everyone agreed it had been a wonderful meal.

"I couldn't eat another thing if you paid me – I might have to employ the two of you to cook for me in the café when it opens," Victor said, glancing from Beth to Aaron and smiling.

"I don't think I could cook for a living. I'd be a bundle of nerves wondering what anyone thought," Beth said, rising to clear the plates.

Aaron rose, too, passing the sleeping Andy to Trina and helping Beth with the plates, even as Kathryn protested.

"You can't do that – you're our guest, Aaron," she exclaimed, but her insistence, quite literally, fell on deaf ears. Aaron soon had the table cleared and was rolling up his sleeves to help with the dishes.

Many hands made light work and soon the kitchen was clean and tidy, the leftovers from the dinner covered and stored away for the next day. It was getting late now, darkness had long since fallen, and the snow was still coming down in big fluffy flakes that seemed to float in the air. Louisa had fallen asleep, and Beth and Isaac were ready to depart.

"We'll take you home in the buggy, Aaron," Isaac said, gesturing toward the door, but Aaron shook his head and made a walking movement.

"I can walk," he said.

"It's all right – the buggy, Aaron," Victor repeated, but it seemed Aaron was adamant he would not go with them in the buggy.

Kathryn brought his coat and hat for him, a worried look on her face. "Are you sure you'll be all right in the dark walking up that awful hill?" she asked, but Aaron only looked at her blankly.

Communication was so difficult, save in its simplest form, and Trina wondered how easy it would be to learn a simple sign language to help her communicate.

"Be careful," she mouthed at him, and he nodded.

"I will," he said, pulling on his coat and hat.

Andy and Louisa were both fast asleep on a chair by the stove and Aaron made his way over to them and looked down at them and smiled. He reached out and put his hand gently on each of their heads, turning to Trina and smiling, as Beth came to lift Louisa into her arms ready to take her home.

"I'm glad you met Andy today," she said, and he nodded as though he understood.

Beth, Isaac, and Victor said their goodbyes, and Kathryn opened the door, peering out into the snowy night. The moon appeared from behind a cloud so that its light brought a sparkle to the snow-covered garden.

"It's a cold night – stay safe out there all of you," she said, as the guests filed out.

Beth and Isaac climbed up into the buggy with Louisa and Victor brought the horse from the stable at the side of the house, attaching him to the traces, before leading him off with a cheery farewell.

"I'll bring the buggy back for Conrad to look at in the morning – he'll be here, won't he?" he called out.

Kathryn nodded. "He's always tinkering with the buggies in the mornings. Come about ten o'clock," she called out.

Trina's uncle had been a buggy repairer, and the workshop at the side of the house was still used for the same purpose – convenient, given what had happened that afternoon. They watched as the buggy disappeared down the lane, and Trina turned to Aaron, who nodded and gave a slight bow, gesturing over his shoulder that it was time for him to leave, too.

"You take care in the snow," Kathryn said, and she smiled at Aaron, who blushed.

"Thank you, for dinner," he said, and she nodded.

"It's the least we could do – you come by anytime you like," she said, and wishing him goodnight, she stepped back inside.

But something made Trina linger on the porch steps, a desire to find some way of thanking Aaron for what he had done. He had saved not only her, but Andy, too, and given what had happened to Melvin, this was surely no coincidence. As the evening had gone on, Trina had sensed a growing feeling of *Gott's* hand in all of this, a providence which had brought Aaron to them at just the right time, and she was keen to know more about him.

"May I walk with you a little of the way?" she asked, gesturing to her feet and pointing along the lane, and knowing that Andy would be perfectly all right in Kathryn's care.

Aaron looked surprised, but he smiled and nodded, offering her his arm as they stepped down from the porch and across the garden. It seemed the most natural thing in the world, and despite knowing him for only a few hours, it seemed to Trina a friendship had already formed. It was born of a near-disaster and the saving grace that had appeared so unexpectedly, but it felt strong already.

CHAPTER SIX

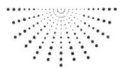

It was not easy to walk and talk in the snow, and far less so given Aaron difficulty in understanding what Trina was trying to say. What she wanted to say was clear enough – she wanted to tell Aaron how grateful she was for what he had done, not only in saving them from the near-disaster of the buggy accident, but for how he had put Andy at ease, and, if truth be told, herself, too. But communicating that to a man who could not hear presented its own problems, as she had found at dinner, and in the darkness of the snowy lane, it was proving harder still.

Trina paused, turning to Aaron, who looked at her and smiled. He had lost something of his nervousness, and now that they were alone together, it seemed he no longer felt overwhelmed by the constant cross of talk that he was excluded from during dinner. The air was perfectly still, the snow falling silently around them, and only the crunch of their boots on the ground broke the stillness. The moon was half hiding behind a cloud, but its light was enough for them to see the smiles on one another's faces, and for Trina to attempt to offer her thanks again.

"I'm so grateful for what you did," she said, making the words slowly and overly exaggerated with her mouth.

Aaron shook his head, unable, it seemed, to understand her. It saddened her to think what his world must be like, trapped inside a soundless existence, whilst around you there unfurled a landscape of sound. She could not imagine life without hearing. It was like sight, or touch – fundamental to understanding the world, a world which was surely far poorer for that loss. At that moment, she thought of how she might communicate differently with him, and on impulse, and not quite knowing why she was doing it, she reached out and touched his face. Despite the cold, his skin felt warm to the touch, and she smiled at him, running her finger down his smooth-shaven cheek.

"You've been very kind," she said.

His eyes opened a little wider and a smile crossed his face.

She had taken off her glove to touch his face, and now she put it back in her pocket to warm up, her fingers touching a notebook she had put there that morning in Pittsburgh, planning to jot down any observations from the Greyhound bus for the poems she liked to compose. There was a pencil there, too, and she struck on the idea of writing down what she wanted to say. She drew them out and held them up to him. He seemed to understand, and she opened the notebook and began to write.

"We are so grateful to you. You saved our lives. We can't thank you enough. And you made us feel welcome, especially Andy. Thank you," she wrote, handing him the notebook, which he squinted at in the moonlight.

A smile came over his face, as though for the first time that evening he fully understood – rather than second-guessing moving lips and flailed gestures.

He held out his hand for the pencil, and Trina handed it to him, watching as he began to write. He was a quick writer, and his script was elegant and neat. When he had finished, he handed her back the notebook, and she read his words, a smile coming over her face.

"I'm so pleased to meet you. I'm only glad I was in the right place at the right time. It was surely Gott's will. Welcome to Faith's Creek. You and Andy will fit in perfectly here. Thank you for your kindness to me," it said.

Trina looked up at him and nodded, her smile growing broader.

In reading his words, it was as though she were being introduced to him for the first time. This was the real Aaron – not a series of gestures or distant words. He was as clear and concise as anyone, and his disability was no barrier to his knowing just what he wished to say. Trina had never met a person like Aaron before. He had a calmness and serenity about him, and it seemed as though he viewed the world differently to other people. As if he were able to see beyond the everyday, his senses – those he had command of – were more highly attuned than others. He fascinated her, and she was keen to know more about him. She took the notebook and scribbled hurriedly in it again.

"I'd very much like to get to know you better, and I'm sure Andy would like that, too. I've visited Faith's Creek many times, but it was a long time ago. Perhaps you'd like

to show us around," she wrote, handing him the notebook again.

It was a strange way of communicating, but it seemed to work well in the present circumstances, and Aaron looked down at the notebook and smiled.

"I'd like that, and during the day, I can lip read more easily. Maybe tomorrow?" he replied.

She smiled, reaching out and taking his hand. "Tomorrow," she mouthed, and he nodded.

They were at the bottom of the hill, and he pointed upward to where the light of a cabin could be seen. That was where he lived, Trina supposed, and she smiled at him, pointing back toward her aunt's house, and mouthing "tomorrow," at him again. Their hands lingered together, and he brought her hand to his lips and gently kissed it. She had not put her glove back on, and the feel of his lips against her skin was warm and comforting.

"Thank you," she said, and he nodded, before turning to walk up the hill alone.

Trina watched him go, thankful for those moments they had spent alone – she had taken a chance to thank him and make that gratitude known. He looked like a lonely figure traipsing off through the snow, and she wondered what thoughts filled his mind, the only voice he could truly hear. He had been so brave that day, and kind, too, a kindness which would surely be repeated the next day. She was looking forward to seeing him again, and she returned to her aunt's house with her spirits lifted, unburdened of some of the worries she had had in agreeing to spend the holidays in Faith's Creek.

"I feel so sorry for Aaron, his hearing gone, and that brother of his, well, enough said about him, the better," Kathryn said when Trina had laid Andy down in the makeshift bed which Kathryn had set up for him in the corner of Trina's bedroom.

"What happened?" Trina asked, looking curiously at her aunt.

"His parents died, and so did his sister – she was always so good with him, but Jeremiah... well, I don't know for certain, but he keeps Aaron under his thumb. He's always out running errands for him, or shopping, or going here and there. It must be a difficult life. Do you want some cocoa?" she asked.

Trina nodded. It saddened her to think of Aaron having such a life. He was such a good person – that much was clear from just a brief encounter – and what an awful tragedy he had endured in losing not only his parents but his sister, too. Trina knew what it was like to lose a loved one, and she wondered if she might do something to help Aaron in his grief by being a friend to him.

"I've not had cocoa in years, not since I was last here, I think," Trina replied.

"I'll bring you up a cup. You get ready for bed – you've had a long day, even without the buggy accident," she said.

Trina was grateful to her aunt for the kindness of her welcome.

She felt at home in Faith's Creek, and after all the worry and the tragedy of the previous months, she was glad to at last find a sense of peace amidst the turmoil. A single lamp burned at the bedside. Trina put on her nightgown and climbed beneath the blankets. The bed was warm and snug, and she glanced over at Andy, fast asleep on the bed in the corner. He was sleeping peacefully, and she smiled to think of the bond which he had made with Aaron and how the two of them had formed a friendship even with only a few words. Andy was just like his *daed* – kind and thoughtful, and she pictured Melvin now, his handsome face and the smile he kept only for her.

"Here's your cocoa," Kathryn said, entering the room a few moments later, but Trina was already fast asleep...

CHAPTER SEVEN

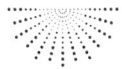

Trina woke the next morning to the smell of cooking wafting up the stairs. Andy was still asleep – a surprise to her, for normally he would wake several times in the night, often crying out for his *daed*. It seemed that the peace of Faith's Creek had affected them both, for Trina, too, had slept soundly. A mug of cocoa sat on the bedside table, and she realized she must have fallen asleep even before her aunt had brought it up. She smiled to herself, stretching out with a yawn. The bed was so comfortable, and from it, she could see through a crack in the curtains that the snow was still falling outside. Despite this, the house was warm, and Trina remembered her promise to see Aaron that morning – she would make the walk up to the cabin, taking Andy with her, and suggest a walk to him. Trina was eager to explore Faith's Creek, for it held so many memories, memories she knew would be a healing remedy to recall.

"Good morning, Trina," Kathryn said, appearing at the door a moment later, holding a cup of coffee in hand.

"I didn't mean to sleep so late," Trina said, hurrying to get up.

"Don't worry – you're not here for anything more than to rest. Beth and Isaac are here with Louisa – they've come to make breakfast. There's blueberry oatmeal, and an egg and potato casserole. You drink your coffee and get Andy ready, then just come down when you're ready, all right?" Kathryn said, and Trina nodded with a smile.

Her aunt set down the coffee and took the cocoa away, and Trina got up, crossing the room to where Andy was still fast asleep on the makeshift bed. He looked so like Melvin, and Trina reached out and swept back his hair, causing him to stir and open his eyes.

"Good morning, little one. Did you sleep well?" she asked.

He smiled up at her, his eyes barely open, his front teeth were still not yet fully through – a toothy smile, as Melvin would have called it.

"I like it here," he said.

"I like it, too. Come on now, let's get you ready," she said, lifting him off the bed and into her arms.

A short while later, after she had washed and dressed and got Andy changed into a clean pair of dungarees, Trina made her way downstairs to find Kathryn, Beth, and Isaac at the breakfast table. Louisa was there, too, and Trina set Andy down on the chair next to her, the two *kinner* looking at one another and smiling.

"I think they'll be good friends, don't you?" Beth said.

Trina nodded. "I'm sure they'll soon be causing all sorts of mischief together," she said.

Kathryn laughed. "It's wonderful to have the house full of *kinner*. It makes me so happy," she said, as Beth set down the casserole dish on the table.

"I hope you're hungry," she said, taking Isaac's plate and serving him a large helping.

The food was delicious and compared to the meager offerings that Trina had been bothered to make for herself in the previous months – ready-made meals and take-outs – it felt like she was staying in the most wonderful hotel imaginable.

"I'm going to pay a visit to Aaron this morning – I'd like to get to know him a little more. I still can't believe what he did for us yesterday. It was so brave – I feel we owe him our lives," Trina said, as she finished her plate of casserole.

"He'd appreciate that. I don't think he has many friends, though Bishop Beiler's been good with him – he always tries to involve him in anything to do with the Sunday services," Kathryn said, wiping her plate with a slice of buttered bread.

"It's his brother that's the problem," Isaac remarked, and again Trina wondered what it was about this man which caused others to pass such comments.

"Is he violent toward him?" she asked.

Isaac shrugged. "I don't know, exactly – but I just get the feeling that Aaron isn't always his own master… if that makes sense," he replied.

Trina nodded. The thought saddened her, though it made her all the more determined to be a friend to the man who had done so much for her and Andy. Once breakfast was concluded, Trina put on a kapp over her prayer covering, grabbed a shawl, and made ready to leave. It felt strange to wear the prayer covering again – in Pittsburgh, she had never worn one, but here in Faith's Creek, it seemed the right thing to do and now she put her overcoat on and bid the others goodbye. Beth had offered to watch Andy – he and Louisa were playing happily on the rug in the parlor, and Trina assured them she would be back in time for the midday meal.

"Take as long as you want – you're not here to work, remember," Kathryn said.

Trina smiled. "I'll feel terribly guilty if you don't let me do something, Aunt Kathryn," she replied, but her aunt was having none of it, and neither was Beth, who reminded her what a pleasure it was to have another *mamm* around to talk to, before bidding her goodbye.

"I'm sure Aaron can show you all around the community – he goes on great long walks by the creek and up onto the ridge. I often see him, though it's so hard to know how to talk to him," Beth said, as Trina stepped out onto the porch and pulled on her boots.

But Trina had found the perfect way to communicate with Aaron – it was just a matter of patience, and sometimes a notebook and pencil which she had made sure was in her pocket, ready for just such an eventuality. The tracks across the garden had already been covered in the fresh snowfall and everywhere looked sparkling and clean, a blanket covering the landscape, and the clouds on the horizon promising further falls that day. Trina made her way across to the garden gate and followed the lane back in the direction which she and Aaron had taken the night before. There was an eagerness in her to meet Aaron that she did not quite understand but she would pray on it as she walked. Gott would lead her in the right direction, she was sure of it.

In the daylight, she began to recognize familiar sights, recalling those memories of a childhood long buried. There was the tree in the center of a field that her uncle had attached a swing to, for her and Irene, and the house across the way was that of the baker, from whom she and her cousin would go to buy warm buns, with chocolate frosting. There were so many happy memories. Trina was glad that amidst the sadness of her current situation, she could look back to something better, and the promise of a brighter future to come.

The cabin stood out against the stark landscape surrounding it. The wind across the hillside had blown the snow into great drifts, and the fences which surrounded the cabin's garden had all but disappeared. It was a stark contrast to her aunt's snug and cozy house, and Trina felt terribly sorry for Aaron that his circumstances had led him to such a cruel existence. The gate into the garden was half-open, and smoke was rising from the chimney so Trina was certain someone was in. The curtains were open, and she followed the outline of a path through the snow and up the steps onto the porch. Several pairs of boots stood there, along with tools on a long bench – they looked ill-kept and blunt. She was about to knock at the door when the sound of a raised voice came from inside.

Trina felt her heart beat faster and a feeling of such profound sadness overwhelmed her. What should she do?

CHAPTER EIGHT

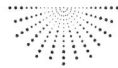

*B*efore Trina could decide what to do the shouting continued.

"What are you, stupid? Don't answer that. I sat here for three hours waiting for you – no food, no word of where you were. I thought you'd had an accident, but no, you were having dinner with someone else, leaving me to starve. What thanks is that for all I do?" the angry voice came through the thin walls of the cabin.

Trina guessed this was the brother she had heard the others speak of.

She could picture Aaron inside the cabin, his brother's hand raised against him. Did he even know what his brother was saying? But there were more ways to communicate with someone than words – the look of anger, the gestures of the hands, the narrowing of the eyes. Trina had to help, she knocked loudly at the door.

There was a pause in the diatribe before it was flung open to reveal a man not too dissimilar in looks to Aaron, though older, but with a face which looked like thunder.

"Oh, I'm sorry. Am I disturbing you?" Trina asked, trying to make her tone suggest she had heard everything.

The man faltered slightly, a blush coming over his face, and he forced a smile to his lips, nodding his head to her and stepping aside.

"And who do we have the pleasure of meeting?" he asked, as Aaron appeared behind him with a broad smile on his face.

"My name's Trina, Trina Peachey. I'm a friend of Aaron's," she said, catching Aaron's eye and mouthing a "hello" to him.

The brother had composed himself – evidently realizing that she was the woman who had caused his brother's absence the evening before.

"I'm very pleased to meet you, I'm Jeremiah Lehman – Aaron's brother and... guardian," he said, holding out his hand to her.

Trina took it and smiled, though she could summon little by way of genuine delight in meeting the man, who seemed the very opposite of his brother.

"It's nice to meet you," she lied, and he beckoned her inside.

"Come in out of the cold. Aaron will make some coffee for us," he said, and Trina was ushered inside.

The cabin was sparsely furnished, though Trina could not help noticing the number of books piled around the room which seemed to serve as a parlor. In the corner stood a stove, and the rudimental fittings of a kitchen, and to the side was a door leading to what she presumed was the bedroom where the two brothers slept. It was nothing if not basic.

She took the chair which Jeremiah now offered her, whilst Aaron went to make the coffee.

"Don't go to any trouble on my account," Trina said, for she could see Aaron cutting slices of seed cake which he had taken from a tin on the shelf, but with his back turned, Aaron would not even know she was speaking to him.

"I'm sorry he caused you so much trouble last night – you were the young lady who took pity on him, weren't you?" Jeremiah said.

Trina shook her head. "I didn't take pity on him – I invited him for dinner. Well, my aunt invited him, but it was no act of mercy. We wanted to thank him for what he did, rescuing us from the buggy. If it hadn't been for Aaron, then we'd have been seriously injured – my son and me, my aunt, and her friend Victor. We owe Aaron our lives," she replied.

It was no exaggeration, and the more she thought about it, the more Trina was certain that the hand of *Gott* had sent Aaron to them in their time of need. She could never truly repay him for what he had done, and now she wanted him to understand just how grateful she was.

"He does impose himself, at times. I have to tell him, not everyone wants to put up with a man like him, but does he listen – well, he can't, can he?" Jeremiah said, shaking his head.

Trina was shocked by these words, and thankful that Aaron still had his back to them and could not hear what was being said. It was dreadful to think of the wicked things which Jeremiah had in mind, and she shook her head and frowned, determined to stand up for the man who had rescued them from near disaster.

"He wasn't imposing himself. Actually, I came to invite him on a walk – I want him to show me around Faith's Creek. It's so long since I was last here, and I understand he likes to go on long walks.

Aaron had returned with the coffee and a plate of cake, he offered it to Trina, smiling at her as she thanked him. She made a point of looking straight at him and slowing down her speech when she talked. He was perfectly capable of understanding, and he seemed delighted to have her there, the smile never once leaving his face.

"Just don't expect too much of him – he's not used to company," Jeremiah said, a scowl coming over his face.

But Trina had made up her mind to ignore Jeremiah, and instead, she fixed her eyes on Aaron as he handed her a cup of coffee.

"Shall we go for a walk today?" she asked, gesturing with her feet.

Aaron nodded, and Jeremiah now rose angrily to his feet.

"Some of us have work to do – work to keep the likes of him. Well, good day to you, and I'm sure my brother will do his best to show you around," he said, nodding curtly to Trina, before turning to his brother.

"I will get the food," Aaron said, his tone nervous as his brother snarled at him.

"You'd better – I don't want to be eating out of a can again tonight. If someone invites you for dinner again, tell them you don't like to impose – all right?" he said.

Aaron nodded.

Jeremiah stormed out of the cabin, slamming the door hard behind him so that the whole place shook. Aaron turned with an apologetic look on his face, but Trina only smiled and beckoned him to come and sit down opposite her. She drew out her notebook and pencil, offering it to him, but he shook his head.

"Sign," he said and made a series of gestures with his hands.

Trina could not understand, and she shook her head in confusion, pointing to the notebook and scribbling down her own words on the page.

"*I came to thank you again for what you did for us, yesterday,*" she wrote, and Aaron nodded.

But the smile was gone from his face, and he glanced at the door and pointed, shaking his head.

"Your brother?" she asked, speaking slowly, and he nodded.

"He took the notebook from her and scribbled quickly over it, handing it to her with an embarrassed look.

"*I shouldn't have stayed yesterday, I'm sorry I imposed on you, and I'm sorry if I was a nuisance,*" it read.

Tears welled up in Trina's eyes.

His brother had caused these feelings and made Aaron believe he was worth nothing in himself. It was so sad to see a man treated like this and made to believe he had nothing to offer anyone. She shook her head and fixed him with a stern gaze.

"You're not to think like this," she said, shaking her head and pointing to the notebook, "it's not right."

He seemed to understand, but he shook his head and sighed, appearing shamed at the thought of what he had done. His brother had humiliated him, and Trina was determined to make him understand the value she placed in him, a value on which his disability had no bearing. She would try her best to learn the sign language, to communicate with him as best she could, and to be a friend to him – whatever it took. They had known one another but a few hours, but the intensity of the experience they had shared had given rise to a bond, one which could never be undone.

"I'm sorry," he said, but again she shook her head and reached out to take his hand in hers.

"You've nothing to be sorry about, do you understand?" she said, gazing into his wide, tearful eyes.

He hung his head and sighed, and she squeezed his hand, shaking her head sorrowfully at the sight of a man so broken by the harsh treatment of his brother that he had come to believe he had nothing good to offer. It was a terrible situation, and the only way to resolve it would be for Aaron to stand up to Jeremiah and make him realize that his harsh treatment would be tolerated no longer. But such things were easier said than done, and from what she had learned from her aunt and Isaac, it seemed that Aaron had long lived under his brother's shadow. Aaron gestured for the notebook, and he scribbled something down, handing it to Trina to read.

"Look at this place. I can't even welcome you properly. It's a mess, and I'm a mess. I feel ashamed for you to see me like this," it read.

Trina shook her head biting back the tears that threatened to flood her eyes. Taking the notebook she wrote back. *"You've nothing to be ashamed of. It's the way your brother treats you – he's the one who should be ashamed."*

Aaron rose to his feet and went over to fetch down a pot on the shelf, out of which he drew a few scrunched-up dollar bills. He held them out to Trina, gesturing as if to say they were all he had.

"Your allowance?" she said, making a gesture she hoped suggested ownership.

He nodded, sadly, and Trina could now understand better the sad conditions under which he lived. He was totally dependent on his brother for everything, and if he put a foot out of line, he would find himself on the receiving end of a vicious tongue. It was no life for him, a pitiful existence, one which the thought of made Trina extremely angry.

"All I have," Aaron said.

Trina shook her head. "I know what it's like," she replied, but he did not seem to understand, and she took up the notebook and wrote something about herself.

She described her situation – the death of her husband, and how she and Andy had come to Faith's Creek in the hope of finding peace at Christmas time. It was hard to write such personal things, though somehow she knew Aaron would understand, and when she handed him the piece of paper, he looked at it and gave a weak smile.

"I lost my parents," he said, and she took hold of his hand and squeezed it.

"We both know what loss is like," she said, and now he did seem to understand, brushing a tear from his eye.

A thought came over her, and she wondered at the possibility of doing something to help him. The thought of Aaron in the cabin with his brother for Christmas was a dismal one, and Trina was certain that her aunt would welcome him into her home for the holidays. After all, they owed him so much. Trina took up the notebook again and scribbled down her plan, handing it to Aaron with slight trepidation. He read it and glanced up at her with a look of astonishment.

"Me?" he asked, and she smiled.

"Yes, you. The holidays – Christmas," she said, and now he scribbled again on the notebook, handing it to her with a smile.

"I wouldn't be imposing?" he wrote, and she raised her eyebrows at him and frowned.

"No," she replied, emphatically and offered him her hand, which to her relief, he took.

CHAPTER NINE

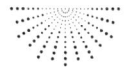

Trina wasted no time in asking her aunt if Aaron could stay with them for the holidays, and Kathryn was only too happy to oblige.

"He could do with looking after," she said, and welcomed Aaron warmly back into the house, sitting him down by the stove and bringing him a cup of cocoa.

Trina knew that Jeremiah would be angry to find Aaron gone, and later that day, she returned to the cabin and left a note there for him, pinned on the door. It told Jeremiah, in the simplest of terms, that Aaron would not be there for Christmas and that he was spending the time with friends – which friends would be up to Jeremiah to decide.

Beth and Isaac were surprised when they arrived later that day with Louisa to find Aaron and Andy playing happily on the rug. They had developed an astonishing rapport and given that Andy was still communicating both in speech and gesture, it was not long before they had created their own sign language, simple, but effective.

"It's remarkable," Beth said, as she set Louisa down on the rug.

"You should have seen the way his brother treated him. It was just awful," Trina said, shaking her head sadly.

"Jeremiah isn't a very nice man – there's few that have a good word to say about him, and I say that as a *Gott* fearing man," Isaac said.

They were to have schnitzel for dinner that night, with potato cakes and cabbage, and Beth and Trina set to work peeling the potatoes, just as Aaron entered the kitchen and stood watching them with a smile.

"Here's the real chef," Beth said, making the shape of a chef's hat over her head and pointing to the pans.

Aaron laughed. He had a nice, gentle laugh, and he rolled up his sleeves to help, just as Andy came toddling into the kitchen. Trina washed off her hands and stooped down to pick him up, smiling at him, as he whispered in her ear.

"We were playing trains," he said, and she kissed him on the cheek.

"You've made a nice new friend, haven't you?" she said, and Andy nodded.

"Can I make something?" he asked, pointing to where Beth and Aaron were now preparing the dinner together.

His words gave Trina an idea, and it seemed an excellent idea for the two of them to do something special for Aaron as a Christmas present – a thank you for what he had done for them.

"Or we could do a special craft with paper and glue? Maybe Kathryn will have some things we could use," she said. Taking Andy in her arms, she carried him out of the kitchen and into the parlor where Kathryn was sitting sewing.

"I know I said it before, but I love having the house full. It brings so much joy, doesn't it," she said.

Trina nodded. "It's lovely, and Andy's had a great idea. Why don't you explain what you're going to do," she said, as Kathryn leaned forward with a smile to listen.

"I don't think I've ever tasted a better schnitzel," Victor said, setting down his knife and fork with a satisfied look on his face.

The plates around the table were all clean, and the dishes empty, so that it seemed everyone had enjoyed their dinner that evening. Victor had come to join them, and with Aaron, there, too, it was quite a gathering. The two *kinner* were sitting happily next to each other, their plates clean, too. Kathryn offered everyone a slice of cherry pie, freshly baked that afternoon by Aaron – who was already proving himself a most able house guest.

"I don't think we can refuse an offer like that, can we?" Beth said, and everyone asked for a slice.

There was cream, too, almost frozen, for it had been stored out in the barn, where the temperature had barely risen above freezing for weeks, and laying down his spoon, Victor again pronounced himself entirely satisfied.

"I couldn't eat another thing – I might just fall off my chair," he said, turning to Aaron, and gesturing to his stomach and lurching comically from side to side.

Aaron laughed, and Trina glanced at him, happy to see him smiling. There had been no word from Jeremiah as to his absence, and Trina hoped that for a few days, at least, Aaron could experience a different way of life, one which would leave him with lasting, happy, memories.

"We mustn't forget the pageant tonight at the schoolhouse. We went last year, and it was so nice," Isaac said, turning to pick Louisa up from her chair as Beth rose to her feet.

"That's right, we'd better get going if we're going to get seats. You're all coming, aren't you? It'll be a lovely occasion," she said, and the others nodded.

Aaron looked confused, and he turned to Trina, who pulled out the notebook and pencil.

"Tonight is the Christmas pageant at the schoolhouse. We're all going. Will you come? It'll be fun? Andy will love it," she wrote, handing the notebook to Aaron, who shook his head and looked nervous.

"No," he said, and Trina looked at him curiously.

The pageant would be fun – Kathryn had told her all about it. It was a time for the whole community to come together and see the *kinner* perform. There was to be a nativity play, and the *kinner* were to sing songs, too. The whole community would be there, and Kathryn had told Trina that Beth saw it as a mark of being a *mamm* that she take Louisa there to see.

"Don't you want to see the *kinner* perform?" she asked.

Aaron looked at her in confusion, and she wrote it down instead, handing him the notebook and urging him to agree.

He started scribbling something else and handed it to her just as the others started getting ready.

"My brother always told me to stay away from such things – I don't belong there, and I wouldn't appreciate it. I couldn't hear what was happening, and he says it's wrong for me to be at such things," he wrote, words which brought a tear to Trina's eye.

This was just another example of the terrible way in which Jeremiah had treated his brother. There was nothing to stop Aaron from appreciating the pageant – he could still see it, and he surely knew the Christmas story well enough to follow it along. There would be costumes and dancing, not to mention the happy fellowship of the community coming together. Trina knew it would help her, and she was certain it would help Aaron, too, if only he would agree to come.

"Don't let your brother's words stop you. We want you to come – Andy will love it and so will Louisa, too. Please come, I'd like it if you did," she wrote and passed the notebook to Aaron, who appeared confused at her show of kindness.

"Really?" he asked, and she nodded.

"I won't take no for an answer. Come along," she said, holding out her hand to him.

He seemed shy, but Trina refused to give up, and with a smile, he nodded and took her hand in his.

"Come on, you two, let's be going," Kathryn called out, and Aaron followed Trina out into the hallway, where the others were all bundled up against the cold winter's night.

Andy looked up at Aaron and smiled, and he reached out his hands for Aaron to lift him up. Trina was surprised – though delighted – and that simple gesture seemed to reassure Aaron that he was wanted.

"Let's go," Beth said, "we don't want to be late."

CHAPTER TEN

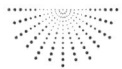

It was only a short walk to the schoolhouse and there was no mistaking the way, for a dozen buggies were maneuvering up the lane, along with a steady stream of parents and their *kinner*. The schoolhouse was lit up, and a path had been cleared through the snow to the door, which stood open to welcome them. Trina smiled to see so many happy faces, the spirit of Christmas filling everyone with expectant joy, and she stayed close to Aaron, who was carrying Andy in his arms.

"Oh look, there's Bishop Beiler and his *fraa*, Sarah. I want to introduce you to them," Kathryn said, as they entered the brightly lit schoolhouse, where rows of chairs had been set out in front of a makeshift stage.

From behind a screen to the left there came the excited chatter of *kinner*. Trina smiled to herself to think of them in their costumes, getting excited for the performance to come. The Bishop was a kindly looking man, quite tall and with a presence to him – a man of *Gott* who commanded respect, his beard long and white, and his eyes twinkling and blue. His *fraa* was very pretty, with a soft, kindly face beneath her kapp.

"Good evening, Kathryn," Bishop Amos Beiler said, coming over to greet them, followed by Sarah.

"I always love the pageant, and I've brought my niece alone. Do you remember I told you she was coming to stay with me for the holidays with her son, Andy?" Kathryn said, introducing Trina, who smiled.

"It's a pleasure to meet you, and it looks like you've got some help there," Amos said, turning to Aaron, who nodded.

Trina was surprised to see the Sarah making signs to Aaron, who nodded and setting Andy down, he signed back to her, the two of them communicating effortlessly.

"Sarah learned sign language after Aaron's accident," Kathryn explained.

Trina watch in fascination as the two continued to communicate.

It was as though they were having an entire conversation, and Aaron was delighting in the ability to communicate so easily.

"I'm so sorry about what happened to you yesterday," Sarah said, turning to Trina, who shook her head, the horrible memory replaying itself in her mind.

"We were just lucky that Aaron came along when he did," she replied, and Sarah turned and explained to Bishop Beiler what had happened.

"I was going to make a point of telling you because he should be recognized for what he did – he's a hero," Kathryn said, Amos nodded.

He reached out and took Aaron's hand, fixing him with a solemn look.

"You did very well, Aaron – we're proud of you, and I'm pleased to see you out and about like this," he said.

Aaron seemed to understand.

The call came for them to take their seats. Trina was pleased to see that Andy wanted to sit on Aaron's lap for the performance. They found seats halfway to the front, and Trina handed Andy to Aaron, who looked at her in surprise.

"He wants to sit with you," she said, gesturing to him.

Aaron looked pleased, and he put his arms around Andy, who lay back and smiled, watching as the first of the performers came onto the stage. The *kinner* were to sing a song first, and the schoolhouse was soon filled with the sound of their voices. Trina was surprised to find tears welling up in her eyes, and she pulled out a handkerchief, dabbing them away, as she thought sadly of what Melvin would miss in the years to come. He would never see Andy in his school pageant, or watch him court or one day marry – it all seemed so unfair, and though she was glad to be there, she knew there would be many moments like this to come. There would be many times when the sadness of Melvin's loss hit her particularly hard.

"Wasn't that just wonderful?" Kathryn said over the applause ringing out around the schoolhouse.

The *kinner* had come on stage to take a final bow, and the schoolteacher was ushering them away, the audience now rising from their seats. Much greeting and well-wishing was going on, and Trina stayed close to Aaron, who had hoisted Andy up onto his shoulders to carry him out. He was certainly a strong man. Trina wondered if he had been a farm laborer or a builder in the time before his accident – certainly, he had great strength.

Andy giggled as he rode on Aaron's shoulders, pretending to be a horse.

"Calm down a little now," Trina said, but Andy only laughed more loudly, and they followed Kathryn to the door, where Beth and Isaac were speaking with Amos and Sarah Beiler.

"I hope we'll see you at service over the holidays," the Bishop said.

Trina nodded. "You will," she replied, and Sarah signed something to Aaron, causing him to smile and nod enthusiastically.

"I asked if he was spending holidays with you – it's lovely to hear he is. Well, goodnight," Sarah said, and she and the Bishop filed out of the hall, along with the rest of the crowd.

Despite her earlier sadness, Trina could not help but feel a sense of contentment at being in the company of friends and surrounded by the celebration of Christmas. It brought a warm feeling to her heart, and she smiled up at Aaron, who lifted Andy down from his shoulders so that they might step out through the door into the snowy night beyond.

"I'm looking forward to a cup of cocoa," Kathryn said, offering Trina her arm.

Trina was about to agree when she sensed Aaron startle at her side.

She turned to him and found him standing ashen in the doorway, his face white as a sheet against the light coming from inside.

"Are you all right," she asked, but he was not looking at her, but instead he looked straight ahead, to where his brother stood menacingly at the end of the path by the gate.

CHAPTER ELEVEN

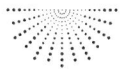

*J*eremiah came striding angrily toward them, and Aaron shook his head, turning desperately to Trina, who instinctively stepped in front of him.

"What's all this, Aaron? What are you doing here?" Jeremiah said, half mouthing, half signing his words with broad, fast, and angry gestures.

Aaron signed something back, and his brother gave an exasperated cry, shaking his head.

"Do you want to embarrass me further? Leaving a note like that, are you stupid?" he exclaimed, gesturing at Aaron, and not even bothering to sign his meaning, the look on his face making it clear enough.

Andy was scared, and he clung to Trina, who now pointed her finger angrily at Jeremiah, the others looking on in disbelief.

"Don't you dare talk to him like that. I've not known you very long, but I've seen enough to know that he deserves better. Don't you ever stop think about how he's feeling?"

Jeremiah looked at her with a stunned expression on his face. "I don't need your advice," he snapped, but Kathryn now stepped forward, too.

"Your parents would be ashamed of you, Jeremiah. And your poor sister, too. They'd have wanted you to take care of Aaron, not treat him like this. We invited him to the pageant, and we invited him to spend the holidays with us. He did a good thing, a good deed in the sight of *Gott*, and for that deserves to be treated kindly," she said, folding her arms.

"You're upsetting the *kinner*," Trina said, as Andy now sobbed into her skirts.

"You come with me, Aaron," Jeremiah said, signing to his brother, who glanced at Trina and then back to Jeremiah.

"You don't have to do anything but what you want to do," Trina said, trying to make Aaron understand.

Aaron seemed to falter for a moment, torn between the desires of his heart and the apparent duty he owed to his brother. Trina felt so sorry for him, the tears welling up in her eyes as she held out her hand to him. But it was Andy who made the decisive move. He held up his arms to Aaron, who looked down at him and smiled, and it seemed that something in him suddenly switched. He lifted Andy into his arms and turned to his brother, shaking his head.

"I don't want to," he said, his words sounding firmer and clearer than any which Trina had so far heard him speak.

Jeremiah was taken aback by this unexpected show of disobedience, and he signed something to Aaron, who shook his head and stepped forward.

"I'm warning you," Jeremiah said, but Aron now faced his brother defiantly.

"I feel happy with them like I did with Mercy," he said, gesturing to the others, who stood in a group behind him.

At these words, Jeremiah seemed at a loss, and he could do nothing but gesture angrily to Aaron, who shook his head and turned away. It was as though something had changed, his once nervous disposition replaced by a resolve to find happiness once again, even if that meant standing up to his brother.

"You did the right thing," Trina said, trying to make Aaron understand.

He smiled at her, still holding Andy in his arms.

"I'm finished carrying you, Aaron – I don't need you, you're just a burden to me, you hear," Jeremiah called out – but of course, Aaron did not hear, and Jeremiah turned and stormed off through the snow.

"What a horrible man," Beth said, shaking her head.

"It's all right, Aaron, you're safe now," Victor said, patting Aaron on the shoulder.

He seemed a little shaken, but there was a look of resolve on his face, and Trina felt proud that he had at last found the courage to stand up to his brother.

"I think we could all do with some cocoa, don't you?" Kathryn said, and the others agreed that was a very good idea, indeed.

Trina was so pleased that Aaron had escaped that awful life but she wondered what would become of him. He couldn't stay in the guest room forever.

CHAPTER TWELVE

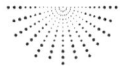

They made their way back to Kathryn's house through the snow. The Christmas pageant marked the beginning of Christmas for the residents of Faith's Creek, and all the houses were decorated for the holidays. A snowman had been built in one of the gardens, a carrot sticking out for its nose, and lumps of coal used to make eyes and a nose. He was wearing a scarf, and Aaron picked up Andy so he could see over the fence and wave to the solitary snowman.

"It's such a happy time for the *kinner*, isn't it?" Beth said as they came to the garden gate.

"The magic isn't only for the *kinner*," Trina replied, glancing at Aaron, who was now holding Aaron in his arms before setting him down on the porch.

"Boots off, and some wood from the store, please, Isaac," Kathryn said.

Isaac nodded and set off to the woodstore, followed by Aaron, who seemed keen to help.

Inside, Kathryn and Beth set to work preparing the cocoa, the two *kinner* – despite it being well past their bedtimes – made straight for the toy box which Kathryn had prepared for them. Isaac and Aaron returned shortly with a good store of wood, and with the lamps lit and the fire kindled, the house was a welcome sanctuary against the cold winter's night. Christmas was coming, and Trina was surprised to find herself looking forward to it.

When the cocoa had been drunk, Beth took the cups out into the kitchen, and Trina got Andy and Louisa ready for bed. The *kinner* would stay the night at Kathryn's house, and they were soon laid down to sleep upstairs, side by side on the bed in the corner of Trina's bedroom. When she came back downstairs, Trina found Beth and Isaac about to depart, though Victor was lingering, tempted by the second cup of cocoa which Kathryn had offered him.

"Well, goodnight. We'll see you all tomorrow. It really feels like Christmas has begun," Beth said, kissing Trina and Kathryn goodnight.

Aaron was nowhere to be found, and after the others had left, Trina went in search of him, finding him, to her surprise, in Kathryn's craft room at the back of the house.

"Are you all right?" she asked, as he looked around at her.

He seemed not to understand, and she repeated herself, sounding out the words slowly for him to understand. He made no response, and there was a sad look in his eyes, almost as if he was beginning to have regrets,

"You did well today, Aaron – you stood up to your brother," she said, fishing in her pocket for the notebook, and scribbling down what she wanted to say.

He read it and sighed, shaking his head, before replying. "I'm glad I did. But I need my brother," he said, hanging his head.

Trina reached out and touched his arm, he looked up at her with tears in his eyes, and she realized what a wrench it must have been for him to utter those words.

Aaron depended on his brother for everything, and without him, his future was uncertain. It was just as Trina had felt before coming to Faith's Creek – afraid of the future which lay ahead. Trina took the notebook and began to write, handing it to him to read a moment later.

"You don't need your brother. There are lots of people who can help you. We'll help you," she wrote, though, at that moment, she was not entirely certain how.

The thought of Aaron returning to his brother simply because he had nowhere else to go was a terrible one, and she knew it would be a sad thing indeed if he was forced back into the life she had glimpsed for a few moments. A life where he was subjected to every whim and will of his brother. A brother who was not a nice man.

Aaron shook his head, but just then, the door to the craft room opened and Victor appeared, looking at them curiously.

"Is everything all right? Your aunt's looking for you," he said.

Trina glanced at Aaron. "Aaron's just a bit upset," she said.

"It's not been easy for him," Victor said. "But there's something I've been thinking about. I had the idea last night, but it wasn't the right time to mention it. Can we talk?" he asked, and Trina nodded, she and Aaron sat down on a couch in the corner of the room, and Victor leaning on the craft table.

Trina felt a strange sensation it was a mix between fear and anticipation. Something told her that Aaron's life was about to change. She prayed it would be for the better.

CHAPTER THIRTEEN

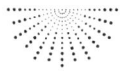

"Should I use the notebook?" Victor asked.

Trina nodded, handing him it, along with the pencil.

He started scribbling, and she turned to Aaron and took his hand in hers.

"You don't have to worry," she said, speaking slowly and over pronouncing the words, but it seemed they were of little comfort. Aaron merely shook his head and shrugged.

Victor finished and handed over the notebook. Trina and Aaron read it together.

"As you know, I'm opening a café in the new year. It's nothing too big, but I need some help in the kitchen. I watched you helping Beth last night with the dinner – you're a wonderful chef, skilled and organized, and I'd like to offer you a job working in the café," it said, and Trina looked up at Victor with a grateful expression on her face.

The offer was a generous one, and it would solve all Aaron's problems – he would not have to rely on his brother for anything and could even think about renting his own place with the money he earned.

"That's ever so kind, Victor. I'm sure Aaron would jump at the chance to work for you," she said, turning to Aaron and expecting to see a smile on his face.

But he only looked at her blankly and shook his head.

"I might have to leave," he said, suddenly rising to his feet, "to leave Faith's Creek."

Trina was astonished by his words. She rose from the couch and caught him by the arm. He was behaving so strangely, and despite Victor's generous offer, it seemed he was intent on returning to his brother – despite the awful way he treated him.

"Wait," she said, but with his back to her, there was no way he would hear her. Feeling lost, she pulled at his arm, forcing him to look at her.

"I'll let the two of you talk," Victor said, hurrying out of the room and leaving them alone.

There were tears in Trina's eyes, and she was surprised by the force of the feelings which welled up inside her. She had known Aaron barely a day, but the thought of losing him – of losing someone who understood something of the pain she was feeling – made her heart ache.

"I don't understand why you can't stay? Isn't this your home? Victor's made you a generous offer, he'd look after you – we all would," she said, forgetting to slow her words and having to write them down.

He looked at the notebook and shook his head, taking the pencil and replying.

I would like to stay, and you've been very kind – you've helped me. But when the holidays are over, you'll be leaving Faith's Creek, and then what do I do? he wrote

Trina read his words, tears welled up in her eyes.

It seemed that he too had experienced an intensity of feelings surrounding all they had shared, feelings that had overwhelmed him, and in that moment, Trina made a decision. She took the pencil and began to write, then handing it to him to read – what it said was life-changing, but the decision felt right – she felt the guidance of *Gott* in that decision.

I don't think I'll leave Faith's Creek. I came here for the holidays, but I've found a home here – even in a few short hours. Everyone's been so kind, I can't imagine going back to Pittsburgh and the life I had here. Andy's happy, I'm happy, and I'm happy to have met you. If I stay, will you?

Aaron read it with a stunned expression on his face.

"I think I would," he said.

Trina felt her heart filled with joy. "Andy's never behaved like this with anyone before," she said, gesturing her words to him, but he shook his head and furrowed his brow in confusion so that she had to write it down for him.

But the smile on his face when he read the words said it all, and she knew she had convinced him to stay. How happy it made her feel to think she had helped him and offered him a chance of a better life. He had been living under the shadow of his brother, just as she had been living under the shadow of her grief, and now she felt she had found someone to understand what it was like to experience such feelings. Trina was certain they could help one another, and she gave thanks to *Gott* for bringing them together in this moment, as Christmas approached.

"*Denke*," he said, and instead of writing down the words she was struggling to express, Trina, put her arms around him, feeling safe and protected in his embrace.

Their friendship had blossomed so fast, but there was no doubt in her mind that it had happened for the right reasons, and that this was the start of something special between them. A week ago, Trina could never have imagined feeling happy again. But now, she felt a glimmer of hope in the future and knew that at long last, there was hope for Andy's future, too.

"It's you I should thank," she said, gazing up into his eyes, neither of them needing words to communicate the feelings in their hearts.

CHAPTER FOURTEEN

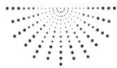

"Oh, there you are," Kathryn said, as Trina and Aaron appeared from the craft room a few moments later.

Trina was surprised to find Andy and Louisa sitting up on the couch by the stove, eating chocolate, and she raised her eyebrows at her aunt, who tutted at her.

"It's Christmas, isn't it? Besides, they woke. Don't tell Beth, but I always let Louisa sit up when she stays over. She loves to help her *grossmammi* with her sewing. But we've been busy, haven't we, Andy?" Kathryn said.

Andy nodded a huge smile on his face.

He climbed down from the couch and ran off into the kitchen, emerging a few moments later followed by Victor, who was still to go home for the night.

"You'll never sleep now, Andy," Trina said, but it was not to her that Andy ran, but to Aaron, holding up several sheets of paper which he presented most solemnly.

"A present," he said, having now learned to mouth the words he was saying and look Aaron in the eyes as he spoke.

"For me? *Denke*," Aaron said, taking the pictures and looking down at them with a smile.

Andy ran back to the couch and buried himself in the cushions next to Louisa. In the excitement of all that had happened, Trina had quite forgotten her promise to make a present with Andy for Aaron, and she glanced at her aunt and smiled.

"He got up to do them – he insisted," she said, shrugging her shoulders.

Trina looked down at the pictures and smiled. The first showed the buggy in the snow, drawn in the naïve style which only a child can manage, and Aaron – or at least

Trina supposed it was Aaron – taking hold of the horse's reins. There were faces looking out of the buggy window, which she supposed were herself, Andy, and Kathryn, with the final figure of Victor peering out the front. The second picture was of the dining table, the family all sat around, and Aaron cooking dinner for them, a big smile on his face, and hundreds of bread rolls all stacked up around him, colored in with crayons. But the last picture needed some explaining. It showed Aaron – or so she thought – clutching a large box filled with kitchen utensils, standing outside a building, on which someone else – presumably Kathryn – had written the word "café."

"Aren't these wonderful?" Trina exclaimed, smiling at Andy, who clapped his hands together.

"But this?" Aaron said, pointing at the third picture, and now Victor stepped forward and smiled.

"That's mine and Kathryn's doing. We're going to buy you all the equipment you need for the café – all the tools a chef needs," he said, but Aaron did not understand, and Trina quickly wrote it down for him, showing him the notebook, and pointing to Victor and Kathryn.

The look on his face was one of absolute astonishment, as though he had never known such kindness. Tears welled up in his eyes, and he turned to Trina and shook his head.

"I don't know what to say," he whispered, the tears choking his words.

Trina slipped her hand into his and squeezed it.

"You don't need to say anything," she replied, shaking her head and gesturing.

"We want to help," Kathryn said, speaking slowly and clearly, and Aaron nodded, still, it seemed, overwhelmed by what they were doing for him.

"Once the new year comes, we'll get you trained up and you'll be a chef," Victor said, and though Aaron shrugged his shoulders and laughed, it was clear he understood the sentiment.

This was Christmas for Trina, the true spirit of what the festivities meant – they had changed Aaron's life for the better and made a difference to his future – to all their futures.

"It's so exciting," Kathryn exclaimed.

Andy clapped his hands together and smiled.

"Did you hear that? Aaron is going to be a chef, just like in your picture," Trina said, and Andy beamed at her.

"Chef Aaron," he said, and Trina took him in her arms and turned to Aaron, who was still looking down at the picture in amazement.

"He drew it for you – this is all for you," she said.

Aaron nodded.

"I think we need a celebration – it might be late, but it's never too late for a slice of cake," Kathryn said, disappearing off into the kitchen, as Victor came forward and took Aaron by the hand.

"We'll make a great team," he said, gesturing to himself and then to Aaron, who nodded.

It seemed that everything was arranged, and when Kathryn returned from the kitchen with a tray of cake and cocoa, Trina announced her intention to remain in Faith's Creek after the holidays.

"If you'll have me?" she said.

Kathryn put her arms around her and kissed her.

"Of course, I will – both of you. This is the best Christmas present I could imagine. We'll be the happiest of families," she said, as Aaron cut the cake, handing around the slices, before putting his arm around Trina with a smile.

CHAPTER FIFTEEN

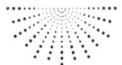

It was long past midnight before the party broke up. Andy and Louisa were fast asleep on the couch, and Victor rose to his feet and yawned, glancing at the clock, and shaking his head.

"I didn't mean to stay so late," he said, as Kathryn rose to see him out.

"Well, we've had a lot to talk about," she said, smiling at Trina and Aaron, who were sitting side by side at the end of the couch.

They bid goodnight to Victor, and Trina and Aaron carried the sleeping *kinner* up to bed. Kathryn had made a room up for Aaron, but Trina was still wide awake, and having laid Andy and Louisa down to rest, they made their way back downstairs, where the last remnants of the cake were on the table.

"What a day," Trina said.

Aaron looked at her with incomprehension, so she took out the notebook and wrote in it for him.

He looked at it and smiled, shrugging his shoulders, and pointing to the pictures which Andy had drawn.

We should put them up somewhere, he wrote, and Trina agreed.

"In the café, once it opens," she replied, and he turned to her and took her by the hand.

"I prayed about this, that I would meet someone like you," he said, his words sounding clearer than normal.

She smiled at him, remembering the many times she too had prayed to *Gott* – prayed for deliverance from the woes which beset her and the terrible agony she had felt in the wake of Melvin's death. Prayer was a strange thing, answered in the most unusual ways. Trina's grief would not just disappear – but it seemed to her that *Gott* had sent Aaron into her life as means to help her deal with it, to accompany her on the road, to share their experiences, and to find a common future. She could already not imagine her life without him, and slipped her hand into his, gazing into his eyes, and knowing his thoughts were the same as hers.

"Shall we pray now?" she asked, bringing his hands together in an arch.

He nodded, and they closed their eyes, their hands still joined. It was a silent prayer of thanksgiving which Trina offered. Thanksgiving for deliverance from danger, and the finding of happiness for herself and Andy. What Aaron prayed for remained a mystery, but she hoped that he too was giving thanks for the good fortune, which was his, and the chance of a new start. When they opened their eyes, he smiled at her, still holding her hands in his, their eyes meeting in a gaze of understanding.

"I feel happy," he said, and she nodded in agreement.

"I do, too, happy that we met – even in the strangest circumstances. I was dreading Christmas," she said, pointing at the decorated fir tree in the corner of the room and shaking her head.

His face fell, but then he raised his finger, a smile coming over his face as though he now understood.

"But?" he asked.

"But I'm not anymore – it'll be the happiest of days," she said, and he nodded, reaching for the notebook and pencil.

She watched him with interest, and he scribbled something down, his face turning bright red in a blush. Trina's curiosity was aroused, and she looked down at the words with interest.

"I want to give you a present, it read, *I want to teach you to sign something."*

Trina nodded, eager to know what it was Aaron would teach her.

He sat up formally and raised his hands, indicating for her to do the same. She laughed but played along, and at first, he pointed to himself, indicating this was the first sign he wanted her to copy. Trina did the same, pointing to herself, and assuming this meant I.

"I?" she asked, and he nodded.

Next, he brought the palms of his hand to his chest, patting at his heart, and she did the same and he smiled and nodded.

"Chest?" she asked, but he shook his head, making the gesture again, and following it by pointing at her, before repeating all the signs together.

He pointed at himself, then placed his palms on his chest, then pointed to her. Trina did the same, and Aaron grinned, even as she looked slightly confused. Kathryn had hung sprigs of mistletoe and holly from the ceiling as decorations, and now Aaron took Trina by the hand and invited her to her feet. She smiled, and he pointed now to the mistletoe and made the three gestures again. Suddenly, Trina realized what it meant, and she blushed, flattered by his words. She looked up at him, their eyes meeting in a loving gaze, and she made the gesture herself, just as he leaned forward and kissed her chastely on the cheek.

Everything about that moment felt right, and Trina could hardly believe the Christmas gift that was hers. She thought of Melvin, and she had no doubt that he and Aaron would have gotten on well, just as Aaron and Andy did. She had arrived in Faith's Creek with no thought to the future, only a desire to heal in the present, but the past few days had begun that healing, and now she had a companion to share it with. How grateful she was to Aaron for all he had done, and now she made the gesture again, determined to learn how best to share their lives together.

"Happy Christmas, Aaron," she said, putting her arms around him, and he whispered the same to her, the two of them holding one another beneath the mistletoe, a happy future awaiting them.

EPILOGUE

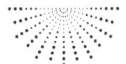

*T*he following April.

Most Amish weddings are held in a barn but this one was different, it was special. The wedding was held in the café that Victor and Aaron ran together. It had a large room at the back and the whole district was there, sitting on the benches reserved for the normal bi-weekly service during the wedding. Well, all accept Jeremiah, he had decided not to come.

The benches had been cleared away and replaced with tables that were laden with a feast including fried chicken, joints of meat, vegetables, and potatoes.

Sitting at the eck, Aaron looked so happy in his suit, his hair smoothed down and a big grin on his face. Trina was wearing a plain Amish dress. In the previous months, she had learned the Ordanung and committed to the church which gave her the right to marry and become a full member of the district.

Bishop Amos Beiler had performed the ceremony in front of the district and Kathryn had glanced around to see that everyone was happy for them. Trina and her son had been accepted as part of the district almost as if she had always been there.

Kathryn looked on so pleased to have seen these two people come together and find love despite the problems that life had thrown their way.

Andy was also so happy, he followed Aaron wherever he went and it had opened him up and helped him to heal. Life for the family was looking on well and Kathryn hoped that it would only get better and better.

The café itself was a success and everyone raved about Aaron's cooking. It had helped him to come out of his shell and to understand that he was not a burden. At first, his brother had tried to shame him to come home. Telling him that people were only being nice to him out of sympathy and that they would soon get bored. Luckily, Aaron had been strong enough to ignore him and his love for Trina had grown quickly.

Kathryn watched as the two on them signed to each other and how Trina helped interpret for him if he didn't understand what was being said.

They were so good together and just glowed with love as they looked into each other's eyes.

Victor came over and sat next to Kathryn. "They make a great couple," he said, "but what about you? Have you ever thought of marrying again?"

Kathryn was a little taken aback, was he asking out of general curiosity, or was there more to it? Up to now, she had never thought of marrying again but what if *Gott* had other plans for her? How would that make her feel, what would she do? No, it was too foolish an idea to contemplate.

Just as she was about to answer Beth came over with Louisa. Kathryn pushed the question to the back of her mind and took the *boppli* in her arms. Life was good, there was no need for change.

If you enjoyed this book, did you miss the first in this series? Grab it here

CHRISTMAS BRIDES AND BLESSINGS
32 BOOK BOX SET – PREVIEW

Trust in the LORD with all your heart
and lean not on your own understanding.
- 6. Proverbs 3:5

✷ ✷ ✷

The air felt crisp and cool, like the sheet of ice that formed over the puddles and pond after the first chill of winter. Hannah Burkholder opened the front door with her left hand and carried the tin bucket with her right. The milk in the bucket sloshed as she set it on the counter. She quickly rushed to the door and shut it, trying desperately to keep the leftover warmth in their small *haus*. It had cooled considerably during the night but it was much warmer than the crisp December breeze outside.

Hannah was filling the last bottle of milk when her husband, Joseph walked into the kitchen. She quickly reached over to a dish on the counter and pulled off the cloth towels that she had draped over it. Before going out to get milk for their morning *kaffe*, she had made breakfast – his favorite.

"Breakfast smells wonderful," he said. Early in the morning, his normally deep voice was a little gravelly and sounded crankier than normal. They were still a young couple, having only been married for a year. However, Joseph's deep voice and aloof personality reminded her of some of the older men in the community – and Faith's Creek, Pennsylvania had its fair share of disgruntled old men.

She smiled sweetly at him. "*Jah,* I've made a breakfast bake this morning," she said. "I know how much you love it."

He sat down at the small breakfast table and nodded. Joseph's eyes moved toward the window as he took a deep breath. "The nights are beginning to get colder.

The morning air feels cooler as well. It might be a harsh winter."

Hannah cut a piece of the casserole and placed it on a plate for him. "It's going to snow. I can feel it in the air. We will have a snowy Christmas this year. I hope that it won't ruin our plans if it gets too bad. We've never had to cancel a Christmas service before."

He let out a chuckle. "You were like this last year. You're as giddy as a child whenever Christmas comes and even more so when it snows." He let out a deep breath. "Don't worry about the service. I'm sure that it will be fine. Bishop Amos will do a wonderful job and we'll both get to enjoy it." He took a sip from his cup.

She sighed. "I love Christmas. There is something about the warmth at the service closest to Christmas Day and the celebration during Second Christmas."

"We're adults now, Hannah. I realize that you enjoy time with *familye* and celebrations but don't you think that you should start looking at life a little more seriously?"

Hannah nodded. "I suppose." She could feel a pang in her heart though for he had mentioned this a few times since they wed two summers ago. She cut herself a slice

"I'll be back for dinner," he said as he put on a coat and took a step toward the door. He paused before opening it. "H-Have a good day," he said. "I'll see you tonight."

"Yes, a good day to you too." She looked at the back of his head and remembered, "Oh, I made you lunch." Hannah took a bag from the counter and handed it to him. "I hope you like it."

He took the bag from her and looked her in the eye. His gaze was often intense and could be somewhat uncomfortable but it was strangely soft this morning. "*Denke*," he said. "I appreciate everything that you do." He kissed her forehead and walked out the door, with the bag in his big, rough hand.

Hannah nearly melted as she stood, dumbfounded, by the doorway. It felt strangely warm in the cool kitchen all of a sudden. The loving gesture was so unexpected, for a moment it made her feel young and innocent once again. She could feel her heart and mind open up a little each day that they were together.

At first, Anna had had her trepidations. When she was younger, she had seen Joseph around the community and both of their families knew each other well. However, she had only spoken with Joseph a handful of times before it was decided that they should wed. She was three years his junior and they had little in common.

He was often cold and emotionally detached. None the less, she tried her best to keep a clean and warm home for him. They talked every now and then but they were never the heartfelt conversations that her parents had. When she approached her *mamm* about it, she merely told Hannah that the love would come in time. They needed to be able to find their place in the community and build their own home first. After that comes love and all the joys that follow it. Anna hoped so for life without love was as cold as the winter frost.

Shaking herself from her dreaming, she quickly put away the rest of the breakfast and adjusted the *kapp* on her head before dusting off her blue dress and walking out the door. As she rushed onto the porch, she double-checked to make sure that her auburn hair was still tucked into place and that she had her favorite sewing pouch in her pocket.

She liked to be the first at the church gatherings so that she could spend a little extra time in prayer before helping with the various tasks that needed to get done. Being a married woman who didn't need any more schooling or to take care of any children, she had the extra time. Some of the other women in the group suggested that before she had any children, she should spend extra time perfecting her sewing and finding her way around the community. There seemed to be a theme though she wasn't really sure what the right answer was or what everyone was getting at.

The sun rose above the hills in the distance, painting the fields with a splash of orange before brightening her world with waves of color and warming the air. Little did she know that the clouds in the distance would end up changing her life so dramatically. The clouds would bring the change that she would need in order to see the path that had been laid out in front of her.

Read this amazing value box set now for FREE with Kindle Unlimited Christmas Brides and Blessings

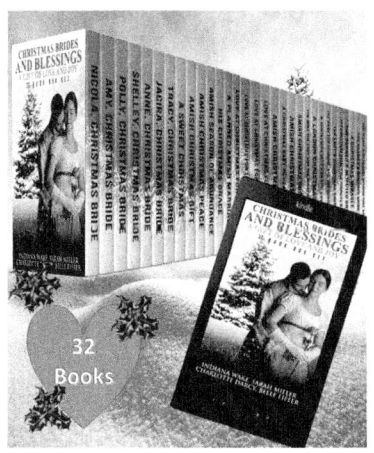

ALSO BY SARAH MILLER

All my books are FREE on Kindle Unlimited

If you love Amish Romance, the sweet, clean stories of Sarah Miller you can join me for the latest news on upcoming books http://eepurl.com/bdEdSn

These are some of my reader favorites:

The Amish Secret Baby Series

Love and Faith

Elizabeth A Baby Blessing

A Baby to Love

A Love Tested

Find all Sarah's books on Amazon and click the yellow follow button

This book is dedicated to the wonderful Amish people and the faithful life that they live.

Go in peace, my friends.

As an independent author, Sarah relies on your support. If you enjoyed this book, please leave a review on Amazon or Goodreads.

ABOUT THE AUTHOR

Sarah Miller was born in Pennsylvania and spent her childhood close to the Amish people. Weekends were spent doing chores; quilting or eventually babysitting in the community. She grew up to love their culture and the simple lifestyle and had many Amish friends. The one thing that you can guarantee when you are near the Amish, Sarah believes is that you will feel close to God.

Many years later she married Martin who is the love of her life and moved to England. There she started to write stories about the Amish. Recently after a lot of persuasion from her best friend she has decided to publish her stories. They draw on inspiration from her relationship with the Amish and with God and she hopes you enjoy reading them as much as she did writing them. Many of the stories are based on true events but names have been changed and even though they are authentic at times artistic license has been used.

Sarah likes her stories simple and to hold a message and they help bring her closer to her faith. She currently lives in Yorkshire, England with her husband Martin and seven very spoiled chickens.

She would love to meet you on Facebook at https://www.facebook.com/SarahMillerBooks

Sarah hopes her stories will both entertain and inspire and she wishes that you go with God.

©Copyright 2021 Sarah Miller
All Rights Reserved
Sarah Miller

License Notes
This e-Book may not be resold. Your continued respect for author's rights is appreciated.

This story is a work of fiction; any resemblance to people is purely coincidence. All places, names, events, businesses, etc. are used in a fictional manner. All characters are from the imagination of the author.

Printed in Great Britain
by Amazon

of her breakfast bake and waited for Joseph to bow his head. Together they said grace before she began to eat.

She looked at her husband, his cheeks were rosy and she knew he had already been out in the stalls. First, he would make sure that the livestock was safe and warm and then he would walk the pasture to make sure that there was nothing wrong with the property. She felt that it was the least that she could do, to wait for him before she took a bite – though she didn't think that he realized she did that just for him.

Throughout breakfast, there were few words said. It wasn't until he had finished that he asked her about her day. "I assume that you're going to help Bishop Amos with the preparations for the district's Christmas service today."

"Yes, it's only four days away and there is so much left to do. I think there is some mending to do as well and…"

"There is mending to do here as well. Don't forget about that." He sounded annoyed.

"Oh, of course not. I plan on darning a few things this afternoon after I get back."